Kiss of Broken Glass

kiss of br

ken glass

by MADELEINE KUDERICK

HARPER TEEN
An Imprint of HarperCollins*Publishers*

HarperTeen is an imprint of HarperCollins Publishers.

Kiss of Broken Glass
Copyright © 2014 by Madeleine Kuderick

www.epicreads.com

ISBN 978-0-06-230656-2 (trade bdg.)

Typography by Erin Fitzsimmons
14 15 16 17 18 CG/RRDH 10 9 8 7 6 5 4 3 2 1
❖
First Edition

To everybody out there
who is aching for the kiss

Kiss of Broken Glass

Tuesday 3:22 p.m.

So here's the thing about being Baker Acted.

You lose everything—
your belt,
your shoelaces,
the perfume bottles in your purse.

They take it all away in the emergency room
and make you sit in the aisle with a box of Kleenex
and a gown that doesn't close in the back.

There's nothing to do except watch the clock
on the wall and wonder how pissed your mom's
gonna be when she gets there.

Tick.
　　Tick.
　　　　Tick.

A cop guards you the whole time,
picks his teeth with a toothpick,
scratches his dandruff,
stares at you like a real creeper.
He talks about you too,

like you're not even there.
To the nurses and orderlies.

"They caught her in the school bathroom," he says,
"using a blade from her pencil sharpener."

A Pruned-up Old Nurse Comes Over

She looks at your wrists and ankles
and the places high on your hips
where it's easy to hide the dark cut lines
even when you're wearing short-shorts.

She's holding a sheet of paper,
with an outline on it,
like a paper doll with no clothes.
She marks up the paper doll
with her fine-point Sharpie,
across the wrists,
through the ankles,
on each hip.

Slash.
    Slash.
        Slash.

You watch that nurse,
and while you're watching
you wish a thousand times
that you'd just waited till you got home
instead of doing it at school where that
Two-Face Tara caught you by the sink—
red drops running down the drain.

You think about the tap of Tara's heels
as she ran to get Mr. Lane and the whoosh
of the bathroom door as he shoved it open wide,
and the look on faces peeking from the hallway—
smirking,
      mouthing,
          busted!

And Here's the Other/Thing
You Need to Know about the Baker Act

Even if
the principal promises
you'll be home before dinner—

Even if
the guidance counselor says
they'll release you right after the ER—

Even if
your teary-eyed mother rushes in
and begs the doctor not to admit you—

"She's only fifteen for heaven's sake!"

It doesn't matter.
You're not going anywhere.
They're gonna lock you up
in a psych ward
for 72 hours.

On My Way to the Ward

Creeper clamps his hand on my elbow,
and it feels rough and prickly as steel wool.

He swipes his badge through keyless locks
and steers me down a pale green hall
where everything smells like fake pine,
and the lights that flicker all look gray.
Then we stop.
It takes half a century for the elevator
doors to open and the whole time we're
waiting I have to lean away so Creeper's
disgusting chunks of dandruff don't
flake off on me.
Inside the elevator it's smaller than a
coffin, and even though I've never been
claustrophobic before, this torpedo of
panic launches in my chest and I try to
yank my arm away and say,

Get your freaking hands off me!

But instead, this stupid sob spills out
and a tear rolls down my cheek,
and there's nothing I can do but

stand there in that flimsy gown
with all my feelings hanging out.

When the Door Opens

I see a sign overhead:
Adler Boyce Pediatric Stabilization Facility.
Someone's scribbled on the wall:
Attaboys Prehistoric Sycho Farm

Creeper pushes an intercom button.
"New patient," he grunts. "Kenna Keagan."

An old woman comes out,
white hair in a bun,
lips tight,
shoulders stiff.

She nods at Creeper
and signs for me on the dotted line
like I'm a package being delivered by UPS.

Then

I step into the ward.

I thought it was gonna look like jail inside,
with steel bars and silver toilets.
But it doesn't.

It's all rainbows and angelfish instead,
painted on the turquoise walls,
glued to the ceiling,
just like kindergarten.

And right away I think,
it's a good thing Avery can't see me now.
This is just the kind of thing my older sister
likes to shove in my face to prove that she's superior.

That—
and the way she looks like
a runway model even in sweatpants.

That—
and the fact she aces every test
with her freakazoid memory.

That—
and the promise that someday
she'll score 2,400 on her SAT,
go to Harvard,
and win the Miss Universe Pageant,
while I stay home and scoop out
my basic B existence
like the plain vanilla,
no topping,
community-college material
that I am.

But I Guess that Figures

Because Avery's only my half sister.
Her dad was some kind of med-school prodigy
who graduated from Johns Hopkins
and probably would've discovered
the cure for cancer if he hadn't died.

My dad's just the backup dad.
The one Mom married afterward
so she wouldn't lose the house on Long Boat Key.
He's an accountant for PwC, which means
he makes good money doing boring stuff
and is hardly ever home.

But I remember this one time
when Dad's client was in Chicago,
he took me and my little brother, Sean, with him
to the top of the Sears Tower—103 floors up.

We climbed into this solid glass skybox
and Sean giggled and danced on the invisible floor.

"Look at me," he shouted. "I'm walking on air!"
And for a minute, I felt like I was too.

We gazed out over the city
where the blue sky meets Lake Michigan
and the sun reflects between buildings
like a cat's cradle of light.

Then my dad knelt down
and pointed toward Lakeshore Drive
and I wanted so badly for him to say,

"See that building?
The one over there?
That's our new home.
Just for me and you and Sean."

Then we'd be so overjoyed
we'd turn into kites
and we'd glide down 1,353 feet
into our new lives.
But that's not what happened.

Instead

Dad muttered something like,
"Too bad your mother and Avery missed this."

Then a cloud passed across the sun
and the city grew suddenly gray
and the cat's cradle fizzled like
a spent candlewick.

Inside the Ward

The nurse who works night shift
waves me over to the counter
with her roly-poly arms.

She's eaten way too many Ding Dongs.

"You're in three B with Donya," she says.
"But don't you act like that rotten girl.
Not if you want to get outta here."

I see a purple Mohawk poke out of the bedroom,
followed by Donya's pale blue eyes.
She waits for Ding Dong to turn her back,
then flicks her middle fingers,
two at once,
double-barreled.

Donya's the kind of girl I like right away.

She slips down the hall and I follow her
to a room where kids are squished in beanbag chairs
watching a flat-screen TV bolted behind thick plastic.

They turn to look at me and I can feel their eyes
crawling on my skin like red ants,

measuring,
    judging,
        labeling,
just like at school.

Then Donya pulls me aside
and tells me how she's been
committed five times
and that the Baker Act
is a giant Epic Fail
just like everything else in Florida.

"I can't wait till I'm eighteen," she says.
"So I can ditch this moron state."

I ask her why she's here—at Attaboys,
and she gives me one of those
zigzag answers that don't say anything specific.
Just that she hates life.
In general.

"You can see how that's a problem, right?" she says.

Then she tells me how easy it is
to hide your feelings around here.

"All you gotta do is *pretend* to be happy.
These Sunshine Suckers eat it up."

Then she tells me to say:

Yes
I'll eat their slimy green Jell-O.

No
I don't mind sharing my life story
with total strangers.

Yes
I'm feeling so much better now.

No
I've never heard voices.

She looks at the bandages on my arm.

"And for God's sakes,
don't say anything stupid,
like algebra homework
makes you want to kill yourself.
Not even as a joke.
There's no jokes in here.
Just reasons for them to keep you longer."

Donya shuts up and motions toward the door.
The night nurse is walking in.

"Lights out, my little bandulus," Ding Dong says.

And it's kind of sick,
but everyone gets up,
without saying a word,
and we follow her down the hall.

Like the good little Baker Actors that we are.

The Whole Time I'm Getting Ready for Bed

Ding Dong stands in the doorway
clicking a pineapple sucker between her teeth.
She takes the soap bar when I'm done,
squeezes a lump of Colgate on my fingertip,
and watches so I don't strangle myself with dental floss.

When she's gone, I open my nightstand
looking for something to read,
but all I find are notes
scribbled inside the drawer.

I want to get out of here

F U Attaboys

Help

Then I lie down on my cold, stiff sheets,
and I kick myself for the millionth time.

You freaking idiot!
Why didn't you just wait till you got home?

And I listen to Donya
grinding her teeth   .
and the sound of traffic
gunning across the bridge,
and I think about all the people
outside our shatterproof window,
coming and going,
        laughing and living,
                hoping and dreaming,
sharpening their
perfect little pencils
and never *once* thinking
about breaking the plastic
to take out the blade.

I'm Having a Nightmare

A terrible dream where I'm running
down a dark country road
and lightning is slashing
across the purple sky.

Then I see this horse.
A gruesome, white, wild-eyed horse.
Rearing in a barren field.
Tearing its flesh on the barbed wire fence.

I bolt awake.
My heart pounding.
Fingers cold.
I look around for my alarm clock,
and the anime poster on my wall,
and the lava lamp I got for Christmas.

But they're not there.

Then, slowly, the room comes into focus,
and I see Donya's spiky hair,
and the rubber-soled socks on my feet,
and the wristband on my arm that says:

Patient #349817

And it feels like my heart stops
as I remember where I am.

Wednesday 8:00 a.m.

It's time for group therapy.
I don't *have* to talk.
But Roger says it's better if I do.
He asks me to go first,
and I decide to get it over with
because pretty much everyone
is squirming in their seats
dying to know what juicy business
brought me to Attaboys.

So I tell them my whole story,
about the bathroom,
and the pencil sharpener,
and Tara the Two-Face.

I'm not embarrassed to talk about it,
because *everybody's* cutting at my school.

Even Tara.

I say how the girls like to compare
their scars
and their slits
and their checkerboard ankles.

We teach each other things, too,
like how to hide pins in our mattress seams,
and steal blades from a dad's double-edged razor,
and how to break bottles in terry cloth
so they won't make a sound.

And we share our best lies,
the ones that will fool any mother—
cat scratches,
bike wipeouts,
shaving nicks.

It's kind of like a club, I say.
Sisters of the Broken Glass.

Roger raises up his hand, stop-sign straight.
He talks about making positive choices
and all that other kumbaya crap,
but nobody's listening.
Donya sticks out her tongue
and I see a silver stud pierced through the tip.
It makes me think about the time
I jammed a sewing needle
straight through my earlobe
without even numbing it.

Pop!

I remember the tickly, fizzy way that made me feel
like drinking root beer on a roller coaster.
And the memory makes something go
click,

    click,

        click
inside my head like a trigger.

I start to fixate on the paper clip stuck to Roger's folder.
The one with all those shiny, sharp possibilities.
I imagine the clip uncurling, transforming,
becoming straight and strong and stiff,
just like an arrow.

A few beads of sweat form on my neck
near the vein that beats faster every time
something really good or really scary is about to happen.

I bet I can swipe that clip when Roger isn't looking,
and I have to bite the inside of my cheek
so nobody sees how excited that idea makes me.

Then I remember what Donya said.
How they can keep me here

even *longer* than 72 hours
for something as lame as a paper cut.

So I sit on my hands
and try to get a song stuck in my head instead,
and send screaming telepathic messages to Roger
to put that freaking paper clip away
before the *click, click, click*
shoots a bullet in my brain.

Have You Ever Tried to Quit?

Roger really wants to know.
He waits for me to answer,
then leans in and looks at me
with eyes so dark and doelike
they make me get all Bambi-ish inside
and for a split second I think about telling him.

But then something coils around me
like a boa constrictor
squeezing,
    tightening,
        crushing,
until I choke out the words to make it stop.

"I can quit *anytime*," I say.
Then I slump back in my seat
and stare at my laceless shoes
and wait for the snake to slither
back into my head.

A Girl Peeps Up from across the Room

"I've tried to quit," she says.

I notice her scarred, bony arms,
her black, bulging eyes,
and the hollow sag of her cheeks.

She reminds me of the baby robin
that fell from its nest two springs ago.
The one I cupped in my hands and fed
with an eyedropper every time it cried:
Mashed potatoes. Egg yolk. Cod-liver oil.

I remember how the fluff disappeared
from the baby bird's head and how
pinfeathers sprouted from its wings.

I'm surprised when Roger says the girl's name.

Skylar.

Like the bright blue sky
on the day I released the robin.

I remember feeling all tangled up inside that day.
Happy to set the bird free. Sad to watch it go.

I think about how enormous that feeling was,
like a balloon blowing up inside my heart,
bigger and bigger, until all I wanted to do was find
a way to let the feeling out before my heart popped.

I think about how I tried to follow the bird with my eyes.
To see where it landed in the tall cypress trees.
But then Avery sprayed me with the hose
and made me jump two feet, and she laughed
when I couldn't find the bird anymore.

"Thank God that little crapper's out of here," she said.

Skylar Flits out of Her Seat

It's all her mother's fault. For heaping
so many unnecessary calories on her plate.
She jabs a finger at her SkinnyJeans.

"I'm *huge*," she says.
"I had to stop eating.
What else could I do?"

Nobody answers.

I look at Roger, with his cheap, coupon haircut
and his brown Walmart shoes, and I wonder
how someone like that could ever help any of us.

But then he does something unexpected.
Something almost promising.

He gets one of those *aha* looks in his eye
and he hops out of his chair,
and for a split second, I feel a flutter of hope.

But then he stops behind Skylar's seat.
Waiting.
Expectant.

Motioning with his hands
like we're supposed to do something.

"Well come on, group," he says at last.
"What do *you* think Skylar should do?"

And that's when I realize
I was right all along.
Roger doesn't have the answers either.

I Get Thirty Minutes of Free Time

But there's no point in free time because
there's nothing to do. I think of all the text
messages piling up on my cell phone.

Holy crap!
WTF?
R U there?

I wish I could answer them.
But my phone is locked
in the secured room,
along with the blade I hide
in the battery compartment.

My stomach starts to knot.

What if Rennie called?
I know she's my best friend and all.
But she gets pissed when I don't answer.
I mean, *really* pissed.

Or what if there's a text about Tara
spreading lies?

Or what if there's a message from
Chase Grayson, the Soccer God,
and he says something
sweet and adorable like

uok?

and I'm stuck in this oatmeal pit,
cut off from civilization,
missing my one and only chance
to talk to the boy I've had a crush on
since the second grade?

If they had to take away my cell phone,
they might as well have amputated my head.

Day Nurse Flaps Her Big Bullhorn Lips

"Exercise time."

I follow her to the rec room.
But there's not much there.
Just some crumbly old floor mats,
a stationary bike, and a treadmill.
It's not like the fitness center back home,
with rows of stair climbers
and elliptical machines
and a rack of blue balance balls
just waiting to be squeezed.

I get on the treadmill and dig in my heels.
The conveyer grinds an inch. Maybe two.
Like there's sandpaper on the bottom of the belt.
When I look up, a boy is standing inches away,
staring at me with his army-green eyes.
I notice his tangled hair, his crooked nose,
and the little scar above his lip that
makes it look like he's about to snarl.

"I can fix that," he says.

I step down and let him yank on the belt
just so I can watch his biceps curl

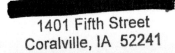

and study the small of his back
as his white shirt rises up and down.

"There," he says, wiping his hands on his jeans.

I feel a little tickle bubble inside. Then I think—
That's the nicest thing anyone's ever done for me.
And if I wasn't already in love with Chase,
I might just give this boy my number,
or maybe I'd ask him to meet me at the grocery store,
in the organic aisle, because nobody shops organic
and it would be sort of private there,
and maybe standing in that secret space
right beside the flaxseeds and granola
he'd lean over and kiss me
with those sexy scar lips.

But I don't say any of that.

I just ask his name.

"Jag," he answers.

And I figure that means his real name
is something embarrassing.
So I tease him about it.

"No way," I say.
"I bet it's Stanley.
Or Leonard.
Or Marion."

And I love how he steps closer to answer me.

"It's Jag," he insists. "For real."

He looks over his shoulder,
makes sure Bullhorn isn't watching,
then bumps the inside of my palm with his knuckles,
soft and playful, until a warm blush crosses my cheeks.

Then he says his name again.
His *whole* name.
And this time it thunders off his tongue
fast and hard like a bullet train.

Jaggernaut Mancuzzi.

And for ten star-spangled seconds,
Chase Grayson ceases to exist.

Room Check

I'm sitting in my room.
Wanting to be alone.
Daydreaming about
Jaggernaut Mancuzzi.

Bullhorn pops her head in the door.

"Are you okay?"

Five minutes later.

"Are you okay?"

Five minutes later.

"Are you okay?"

Five minutes later.

Are you freaking kidding me?

Drawing for Distraction

We're allowed to draw at Attaboys,
which just goes to show how stupid they are
because a pencil is way more dangerous than a toothbrush.

My yellow #2 is whispering to me.
About that pretty pink eraser tip.
I can almost smell it.
The scent of rubber on raw skin.
I imagine slipping my arm under the table
and rubbing the eraser
faster
      faster
            faster
until my arm catches fire
and the skin splits open
and blistery liquid
drips down
to my elbow.

Like mercy.

But I don't do it.
Even though I want to.
Because Rennie says eraser burns are for losers.

I Decide to Draw Instead

At first my lines are soft and gentle.
A wispy willow branch weeping
at the corner of the page.

But then my strokes grow heavy.

I draw a girl with eyes closed, chin down,
and lips sealed in the smallest of pouts.
Her arms end abruptly at the wrists
and her legs trail off just below the knees.

A body unfinished.

"Is that you?" Skylar asks.

I shake my head no.

"I wish I could draw like that," she adds.
"I just write. Poetry mostly."

I tell her I'm no good, but she doesn't let up.

"You could be the next Salvador Dalí," she insists.
"You know? The guy with those melting clocks."

I do know.

I know a lot of crazy things about Salvador Dalí.
Like how he was afraid of grasshoppers
and how he kept mustaches in a cigarette case
and how he slept with a spoon in his hand
so he'd wake up to the clatter of tin
and remember all his dreams.

I know he had freaky dreams too,
with tiger-eating fish,
and giant eyeballs,
and full-grown men
hatching from elastic eggs.

And I know about *The Temptation of Saint Anthony*.

That's the painting with the gruesome, white,
wild-eyed horse rearing on stilted legs.

I feel the hairs rise on the back of my neck
as my own dream begins to resurface.
I try to push it down, but it's like holding
a basketball underwater—
slippery, buoyant, strong.

It won't go away.

I curl my fingers around the edge of the paper
crushing the corner as I clench my pencil tight.
Then instead of sketching hands and legs and feet
in all the places where the girl's body is interrupted,
I make dark, dripping lines that
bleed
    off
        the
            page.

My Favorite Place at School

Is the bathroom.

I draw there, too.
In the extra-wide handicapped stall
where I can rest my head against
the cool maroon tiles and line up
my pens like little soldiers.

It's quiet in there and peaceful
with a sliver of light
that shines through the window.

It's okay to be myself
in that handicapped stall,
even if being me feels
sort of like a blank piece of paper.

I don't have to come up
with any colorful lies in there,
or force a smile until my cheeks hurt,
or roll up my long cotton sleeves,
and show off my scars,
just to fit in.

If Only

I'd eaten my lunch there yesterday.
In that handicapped stall.
Instead of going to the cafeteria
and sitting at the back table with
all the Rennie wannabes.

Then I wouldn't have heard how they cut
while their mothers got manicures
and how they burned squares in their skin
using salt and smooth ice.

If only I'd looked the other way
when they took off their bracelets and
lifted the cloth of their tight cotton camis.

Then I wouldn't have seen
the angry, square welts
or the crisscross of red
that triggered me so bad.

If only I'd put in my earbuds
and cranked up the volume
to drown out the gnats buzzing

cutcutcutcut.

Then maybe,
I could've left school
on the 340 bus
instead of in a squad car
wearing zip-tie plastic handcuffs.

If only.

Oh, and by the Way

You can't trust anyone.
Especially not guidance counselors.
Like the phony hair flipper who acted
all buddy-buddy in the backseat
of the squad car but then left me
with Creeper in the emergency room.

She made all kinds of promises like:

You can go home as soon as your mom comes.

But I bet she knew all along that I was hosed.
She probably signed those Baker papers herself,
right next to the rent-a-cop who dragged me
out of the bathroom and the prehistoric principal
who couldn't stop staring at my arm.

So that just goes to show.

Even if someone says things like:
I feel your pain.
I've been there too.

And even if that someone
wears Aéropostale and still has pimples.

And even if
she puts her arm around you
and makes you feel good for a whole wide minute.

It's all an act.
She's full of it.
Just like everyone else.

One Phone Call a Day

That's all we get.
My mother sounds annoyed
when she answers, and that
makes it almost impossible
to put on my Oscar-winning
two-ounce voice and say:

"I want to come home."

She doesn't talk at first,
and I pinch the metal cord
between my fingers
like I'm trying to wring
the answer out of her.

"It's out of my hands now," she says.
"There's a legal process to follow.
A psychological evaluation.
A family meeting.
A 72-hour mandatory hold."

I wish my mom would say she's sorry
so I could wrap her words around me
like a towel still warm from the dryer.
But she doesn't.

Instead, we talk about orange juice pulp,
and scrambled eggs, and how Dad reacted
when she told him I was here.

I can just imagine that conversation.
Mom with her hand on her hip,
elbow out, like a bossy teacher.
Dad on the other end of the line,
shoulders slumped, like Piglet.

"Kenna was caught cutting at school today," Mom says.

"Which class?" Dad asks.

Then Mom rolls her eyes. Roller coaster big.
Like Dad's a complete idiot.

"Not cutting class," Mom says. "Cutting *herself*."

Sometimes I Wish Dad Wasn't So Clueless

Then maybe he would've noticed
the twisted black hair ties wrapped
around my wrists like bracelets
and the leg warmers that
covered my ankles in June.

And then maybe he would've realized
that hair ties and leg warmers aren't
some new fashion trend
and he would've demanded
that I show him all that hidden skin
and chased me up the stairs
when I stomped off screaming
how it was none of his business,
and pounded on my bedroom door
when I slammed it in his face
and ripped it off the hinges
just like Superman
to save me.

I bet I wouldn't even be here now.

If I had a dad like that.

Dad Used to Have a Little Superman in Him

Like the year Mom drove to Johns Hopkins
so Avery could visit her dead dad's family,
and talking about a dead dad was so fun

they stayed all summer and never wrote,
which is why *my* dad decided
to take me and Sean away.

I remember how he would crank
up the engine on this
old, rented motor home

and we'd drive till we burned
up like two tanks of gas,
and we'd pass the RV park

and pull off the highway on impulse
just to follow some dirt road
that led to nowhere.

Then we'd watch like a million identical
stars wink at us from the sky
for finding their secret spot,

and Dad would give us a glass
of bubbly white-grape juice
for pretend champagne toasts,

and he'd do these stupid card tricks
where the ace disappeared
and Sean couldn't stop laughing.

There was no mother-father fallout
for skipping the five-star hotel
and sleeping on pine needles.

And everything was absolutely perfect
until Dad turned around
and drove us back home.

That Was the Last Time

I dreamed about Dad being Superman.
Or flying off the top of the Sears Tower.
Or driving an old RV into a brand-new life.

Because somehow I just knew
we would always come back.
No matter what.
And that meant Dad would be Piglet forever,
and I would always be the bottom of Avery's shoe.

I didn't realize it back then,
but I guess it's kind of true,
what that poet said.

How once you lose your dreams,
it's like a snowstorm rolls in,
even if you live in Florida,
and the fields freeze over,
and you feel like a bird
with broken wings,
until pretty soon
you can't even
remember
how to
fly.

At Least Sean Still Has ~~Dreams~~

He's gonna be a marine biologist one day.
But he's not like most eight-year-olds
who want to be a biologist today,
a firefighter tomorrow,
an astronaut the week after that.

Ever since his Cub Scout troop visited
the Tampa Aquarium, he's been saying
he's gonna be a biologist and that was
almost two years ago.

Anyway, he's always talking about
these random deep-sea creatures
he sees on the Discovery Channel,
like the Atolla jellyfish that lives
thousands of feet underwater
in total blackness. But whenever
it wants to, the Atolla can turn its
body into a big blue lightbulb,
and not the Kmart special kind,
but a beautiful, brilliant blue.

Glowing.
Luminous.
Unexpected.

Sean says when it happens,
the whole sea stops to watch,
and God looks down and smiles,
because that jellyfish
just goes to show
there can be light
even in the darkest places.

But what does he know.

He's only eight.

Wednesday 11:30 a.m.

I plop down on the couch
to watch a daytime talk show
through that scratched-up Plexiglas.

Donya's yelling HOOYAH
every five seconds because
there's this girl on the show
with a coin-round face
and hair the color of pennies,
who just told her boyfriend
she doesn't love him.
Never did.

Even though he's the kind of boy
most girls would drool for.

Even though he's got eyes
like slices of summer sky.

Even though he can sink a free throw
all the way from center court.

None of that can make her love him,
not for all the corn in Indiana,
because she's in love with someone else.

A girl.
A girl who's like cinnamon apples.
Spicy and sweet.

"I knew it," Donya says.

She hops off the couch and struts
around the room with her boobs
flat as pancakes in that ultratight
underarmor sports bra.

"Hooyah.
          Hell, yeah!"

But when the girl's father appears,
Donya starts to grind her teeth
just like she does at night.

"Parents are hazardous to your health," she says.

She twists her plastic wristband
around and around
until I see the red letters
printed on the underside.
The ones that say *suicide watch.*

"What are you looking at?" Donya asks.

But before I can answer, she's up in my face.

"I wasn't trying to kill myself," she says.
"It was just a buzz gone wrong.
That's all."

I nod and tell her that I get it.
That I believe her.
Even though I don't.

Then we flip through the channels
until that fat Hoosier daddy
is booed off the stage.

Wednesday ~~After~~ Lunch

I notice a piece of paper on the wall
with those little tear-off tabs
dangling from the bottom.

The paper says:

ARE YOU LOOKING FOR SOMETHING?

TAKE WHAT YOU NEED.

And the tabs say words like:

Love
Acceptance
A second chance

I look around to see if anybody's watching.
Donya and Jag are arm wrestling.
Skylar's dumping her uneaten tray.
Nobody's paying attention.
So I pull off a tab.

It feels strange in my hand.
Oddly heavy.
Like the paper is holding
something bigger than itself.
The same way an acorn
holds a full-grown oak tree
inside its tiny shell.

I want to put it in my pocket.
But then I stop and think.
What if this idea sprouts?
What if it gets pink and purple with promise
but instead of growing strong like an oak tree
it just flops over and dies like my coleus plant
in the first grade and leaves me with
nothing but a dead word
and a Styrofoam cup filled with dirt?

Screw that.

Which One Did You Pick?

Skylar flits over and points
at the frayed edges of paper
where three tabs are missing.

"I picked *will power*," she volunteers.
"And *discipline*.
And *self-control*."

Her arm is outstretched, and for the first time
I can see her wormy scars close up.
They look like pink leeches sucking on her skin.

I'll never get like *that*, I think.

My cuts are so much prettier.
Thin as spider silk.
Laced around my wrists like bracelets.

In a week they'll start to heal
and I'll watch as they fade
from rubies,
to ripples,
to smooth opal skin.

When they're gone,
I know I'll miss them.

I wonder if Skylar ever had cuts like that.
Pretty as pink pearls.
Before the leeches came.

She Notices Me Staring

I look away
but not fast enough
and her fragile smile melts.

"Sorry," I say.
"I've just never seen scars
like that before."

She studies me.
Traces a finger across her arm.
Tells me they're her babies.

She's even got names for them.

Fat baby.
Ugly baby.
Lonely baby.
Failed-a-test baby.
Dissed-at-school baby.
Argued-with-mother baby.
Why-don't-you-just-kill-yourself baby.

My cuts don't have names like that.

But if I gave them names, they'd all be Rennie.

Rennie

Where do I begin?

I guess we met around
the second week of sixth grade.
Right about the time I was discovering
that in middle school there's no such thing
as being a wallflower.

You're either popular or ridiculed.
Accepted or abandoned.
Worshiped or crucified.

There's no in-between.
No place for invisible.
Nowhere to hide.

I was a little unprepared for that,
having been a houseplant all my life.
Comfortably nonexistent.

But Rennie took me in.
Introduced me to the black-booted,
purple-haired dress-code violators
who would one day be
the Sisters of the Broken Glass.

And for the first time,
I belonged to something,
  was seen as someone,
    was popular somehow.

I belonged . . .

Even though I knew that meant
I'd have to cut too.
Sometime.

Six Months Later

Elbow on the sink.
Right hand trembling.

Drag-----the-----glass-----across-----my-----wrist-----

chalky-----dotted-----lines-----

don't-----even-----break-----the-----skin-----

Lungs are feeling tight.
Heart is thumping hard.
Rennie's words are swirling in my head.

Just one cut to feel alive . . .

And Then

Whoosh!

The skin tears
and I feel this rush
swirling in my brain
like a waterspout.

A finger-tingling,
tongue-numbing,
heart-pounding
rush.

And the pain doesn't feel like pain
but more like energy
moving through my body
in waves.

Rushing.
    Cleansing.
        Pulsing.

Purging all the broken bits out of me
like a tsunami washing debris to the shore.

Afterward

I feel the calm,
the bliss,
the sheer weightlessness
of zero worry.

I'm floating on a smooth glass pond
with bottle-nosed endorphins
swimming all around,
splashing their tails,
smiling their perpetual smiles.

And I want this feeling to last forever.

Because if the feeling lasts,
it won't matter what Avery says,
or what my mother doesn't say,
or how twisted I feel inside.
Because I know for sure
that on this calm, tranquil pond
nothing and I mean *nothing*
can ever make a ripple in my heart.

But here's the bad thing:

The feeling doesn't last forever.

It *never* lasts forever.

In fact, it barely lasts ten freaking minutes.

Before the guilt sets in.

I Guess That's Why I Picked the Word

Hope.

Because part of me really hopes I can quit.
So I can stop feeling guilty all the time.
Like when I'm washing laundry in secret.
Or wasting my allowance on sterile gauze.
Or lying to my little brother, Sean, about
why I can't go swimming with him.

Those are the times I fumble around
looking for *hope*.

I *hope* Rennie will still like me if I quit.
I *hope* I can stop wearing concealer on my arms.
I *hope* Bio-Oil really works.
I *hope* I won't miss my scars (too much).

But then I remember those ten mind-blowing minutes,
and I think about how it feels the next day,
when everyone crowds around me at lunch,
looking at my cuts, rubbing my shoulders,
dabbing me with *I-feel-so-bad-for-you* ointment.
And I remember the spotlight of Rennie's grin
and the way her approval makes me feel special,

and I gotta say, that's a pretty ginormous feeling.
Like an over-the-top, Sears Tower kinda high.

And just thinking about that
makes my little wad of hope
feel like a spitball
slipping through my fingers
103 stories down
to the bottom
of
my
pocket.

Wednesday 3:22 p.m.

It's been 24 hours since I got to Attaboys.
Donya says they have to give me
my official psych evaluation
in the first 24 hours,
or they'll have to let me go.
That's part of the Baker Act.

I guess that's why Roger's waving me over now.

He introduces me to this pinched-up
Pomeranian face with a clipboard.

Dr. Annoyed-to-Meet-Me
doesn't even look up.
She just drones off
the same pointless questions
they asked in the ER.

1.   Do you know why you're here?
2.   Do you think you need to be here?
3.   What would you do if we let you out?

Hmmm. Let me see.

I'm here because Tara the Two-Face
is a big drama queen who peddles gossip
like Girl Scout cookies, and opening
that bathroom door was like selling
a thousand boxes of Thin Mints.

Do I think I need to be here?
Are you kidding me?
NO. I don't need to be here.
But this works perfect for Tara,
because she'd do *anything*
to have Rennie all to herself.

And what will I do when I get out?

First off, I'm gonna strangle Tara
with a fat wad of dental floss,
now that I know how dangerous
waxed string can be. Then I'll friend Jag
on Facebook and reblog a few GIFs
for my vast audience of Tumblr followers.
All three of them.

After that, I'll ride my bike to Rennie's
and we'll raid her mother's bathroom,
paint our nails Lincoln Park after Dark,
and drink Monster until we get a caffeine buzz.

I want to tell the Pomeranian
that's what I'm really thinking
just to see the look on her face.
But Donya warned me,
it isn't worth it.

So I give her one of those
fake, elastic smiles
and deliver my best lines of BS.

"I'm here because I made an impulsive mistake.
But I'm feeling much better now.
And it will never happen again."

Then I do a little curtsy-bob with my head
and the Pomeranian bubbles in her stupid
Scantron sheet and trots away.

Donya Catches Me in the Hallway

"Not bad," she says. "Might even get you out.
Unless . . ."

"Unless what?" I ask.

Donya snaps her gum
and loops the pink strand
around her finger slow as taffy.

"Unless you got good insurance," she says.
"Then you're screwed."

I follow Donya down the hall.

"What' d'ya mean I'm screwed?"

"Cha-ching," she sings.

I stare at her, my face blank,
like she just spoke Egyptian.

"Oh, come on, Kenna," she says.
"Don't you get it?
If you got good insurance,

they're gonna milk it.
Take their time with you.
Find your inner child
and all that crap.
But with no insurance—
Voilà!
You're miraculously cured.
Sometimes the same day."

I don't want to believe her.
But Donya knows this place like the inside of her pocket.
And if Donya says I'm screwed, then I probably am.

Speaking of Being ~~Screwed~~

At my school, *nobody* narcs on cutters.

Not the goody-two-shoes
who pretend they don't notice
and turn their heads the other way.

Not the stoners who can barely
raise their eyelids.

Not the jocks who are too busy
growing tumors on their arms.

Not even the jerks who call us
emos and *attention whores*
under their breath.

Nobody.

So that makes Tara the first
narc in history to go running off
to "get help" just because
someone needs a Band-Aid.

Only that's not why she did it.

Tara did it because she's a freaking
competitive cutter who can't stand it
if anyone has better scars than her,
and she got it into her head that
people were paying more attention
to me than to her.

That's crap, of course.
But that didn't stop her.

And now that I'm gone,
she'll *own* fourth-period lunch,
with her duct tape bandages
and her six-inch slits,
and she'll be a freaking rock star
just like she wants.

I Wonder What Rennie Thinks

Does she think that Tara's
a two-faced greedy bitch
for ratting me out?

Or that I'm a dumbass
for getting caught?

It's a very tricky relationship.

The three of us.

I remember how one time
my math teacher spent the whole
period talking about triangles.
How they're the strongest shape,
and that's why they're used for building
bridges and trusses because they won't
geometrically distort, or some crap like that.

But as usual, school has nothing to do
with real life because if you ask me,
triangles are the weakest shape of all,
ready to blow apart at any minute,
especially when the three corners are

Rennie,
Tara,
and me.

If Sean Was a Shape

He'd be a circle.

Pure.
Honest.
Perfect.

You can trust a circle.

It doesn't have any crooked angles
hiding secrets in the corners.

It's the same with Sean.

Sure. He can be annoying
when he blurts things out
like little brothers do,
but at least he says
what he means.

He's not a liar.
Or a fake.

I bet you could search
a thousand classrooms,

and cafeterias, and gymnasiums,
and never find that kind of honesty
anywhere else. Believe me. I've tried.

I think Sean may be
the last circle on earth.

Wednesday 4 p.m.

It's bad enough we have to spill our guts
at 8 a.m. when any normal teenager
would still be hibernating.
But apparently one gut spill per day
is not enough for Attaboys.

So when the afternoon rolls around,
they herd us back into the therapy
room for another session.

The only good thing is that Jag's
sitting six inches away from me
in his Screaming Zombies T-shirt
and I can smell the faint woodiness
of skateboard on his skin.

Jag reaches his arms back to stretch,
and it's like every muscle in his body
is in perfect, rippled balance,
and I can just imagine
how good he looks on his long board,
pivoting his Levi hips,
flexing his marble six-pack,
surfing the smooth cement

with his arms long and low
like fighter-plane wings.

He catches me staring at him
and smiles with that half-broken grin
until I feel so sweet and tickly inside, it's
like I'm swirling in a cotton candy machine.

Too bad Roger has to ruin it.

Tap, Tap, Tap . . .

Roger drums his pen on the whiteboard
like he wants to knock some sense into us.
He says we should talk about having goals,
because that's what all adults think we need.
Goals and college plans and career objectives.

But what do they know?

I mean, who says their world is *right*?
What if our real purpose on earth is
something as simple as

Have fun.
Feel good.
Be free.

If it is, then 99.9% of all adults
are failing miserably on this earth,
and when they die they'll probably
be reincarnated as boring worker ants
because that's about all they're good for.

I almost feel sorry for Roger.
Not because he's going

to be an ant in the next life,
but because he really believes
the crap he's writing on the board.

TOP THREE REASONS FOR HAVING GOALS:

x   GOALS KEEP YOU FOCUSED
x   GOALS GIVE YOU PURPOSE
x   ACHIEVING GOALS IS SOMETHING TO CELEBRATE

He says it's best to write your goals on paper,
and he hands us a yellow sheet and a felt-tip pen.
I know I should play along and scribble something like:

x   Quit cutting
x   Get straight As
x   Join a club

But that would be too easy.
And then someone might expect me to do it.
Besides, who can think about goals
sitting six inches away from Jag's lips?
Those soft pink pillow puffs,
dreamy as clouds and totally kissable.

So that's the first goal I write,
in microscopic letters:

Lock lips with Jaq Mancuzzi.

Then I notice Skylar
looking even thinner
after three peas for lunch,
and I scribble down another goal:

Buy Skylar a jumbo burger.

Finally Donya catches my eye,
pretending to walk with a cane,
like that's how old I'll be
when I get out of Attaboys.

So I smooth out my paper
and write my last one:

Blow this place!

And Roger is right.
It *does* feel good to have goals.
Right up until the time
he comes around and collects them.

Waiting and More Waiting

I wonder how long you can sit
in a folding chair before your spine
actually fuses to the metal.

Or how many Nemos
you can count on the wall
before you want to bang
your head against it.

As much as I hate the idiotic
group sessions, the time in
between is even worse.

It's a million shades of boring.

The only entertainment, besides
zoning out to *Judge Judy* reruns
or watching Bullhorn pluck her lip hairs,
is when we get a new arrival,
like the little head case
who rolls in right after group.

He's about the same age
as my brother, Sean.
Eight. Maybe Nine.

Supposedly, he jabbed
his teacher with a pencil.
But looking at him now,
crumpled in a ball on the floor,
he doesn't seem dangerous to me.

It makes me wonder,
isn't there something else
for an eight-year-old?
Like a ten-minute time-out,
or no recess,
or "Sorry, kid,
you lose your lollipop."

Do they really have to Baker Act him?

Seriously?

And when he opens his mouth, I realize
he doesn't even speak English
because he's all, like,
"lo siento, lo siento, lo siento"
but nobody's listening
to the little stabber
no matter how many times
he says he's sorry.

They try to lift him to his feet
and he goes sort of wild,
kicking and spinning,
knocking Ding Dong's
sucker jar off the counter.

The orderlies swoop in
and loop this long white jacket
around him until he looks
like a caterpillar in a cocoon.

When they cart him off,
the only thing I can see
are his tiny inchworm eyes
crying out for help.

And it makes me think:

I don't know why you
stabbed your teacher, kid.
But I sure hope you got her good.

It's Almost Time

I'm staring out the window.
Tapping on the glass.
Trying to remember the last time
I actually wanted to see my mother.

Tap.
    Tap.
        Tap.
Nope.
Nada.
Nothing's coming.

Visiting Hour

Okay.
Maybe I shouldn't have rolled my eyes
at the very first question Mom asked.
But—"How's the food?"
Like I'm at summer camp?
Please!

And now Mom's going through that whole
breathe-deep-and-count-to-ten crap
like it says to do in the tough-love book
she always forgets in the bathroom.

Before long, she starts quoting chapter three:

"Blahblahblahblahblahblahblah . . ."

And then there it is:

Bad choices.

I knew she would say it.
That's the book's favorite phrase.
She grits it between her teeth
like a fat wad of bubble gum

so the other words won't slip out.
The ones she really wants to say.
Like how I'm such a huge disappointment
and why can't I be more like my sister?

I want to tell her,

Hey Mom, I've got news for you:

A hard-boiled egg instead of chocolate cake?
(*That's a bad choice.*)

Vampire Diaries instead of *Supernatural?*
(*Bad choice.*)

Plastic instead of paper?
(*Bad choice.*)

But shredding your arm with a razor blade
and getting Baker Acted like a psycho?
That's not a *bad choice*, Mom.
That's a freaking disaster!

But just when I'm about
to go off on her, I start to feel it.
The way my cuts tighten up

like Grandma's arthritic fingers
right before a storm.

I guess I should've mentioned
how my scars can tell the weather.

Only not hurricanes or tornadoes.
More like the emotional weather.
Like when Mom's waterworks
are about to spill.

So even before it happens,
I know her lips are gonna quiver
and the creases on her forehead
are getting ready to bunch up.
And then out comes the downpour.
A torrential ten-Kleenex typhoon.

Luckily her crying sort of waters down
the rest of the tough-love words:

Foolish.
Dangerous.
Serious consequences.

After a while, the storm blows over.
Mom's hands puddle in her lap

and her head droops like a branch
still heavy with rain.

Great.

Now I'm gonna have to hug her and shit.

And when I do, she's probably gonna
whisper that question in my ear.

The one I can't answer.

Why, Kenna? Why?

Deep, Dark Secret

It would be so much easier if I had one.

Like if I thought I caused
    my brother's illness,
        my boyfriend's suicide,
            my parent's death.
Like if I had
    an alcoholic father,
        a bipolar mother,
            a secret abortion.
Like if I'd been
    molested,
        abused,
            stalked.

Like just about ANYTHING!

Then maybe this would make more sense
and I could answer the question—

Why?

But here's the thing.

I don't have any deep, dark secrets.
Not like that anyway.
My life's not some riveting novel
where you rush through the pages
to get to the end and find out
what horrific, repressed memory
caused me to cut.

The fact is,
I've had a pretty ordinary childhood.
Boring? (*Yes.*)
Predictable? (*Yes.*)
But stitch-worthy? (*No.*)

So I guess that brings me to the *real* secret.
The deepest, darkest kind there is.

I've been cutting for absolutely no reason at all.

And That Makes It a Billion Times ~~Worse~~

Because that means I'm just a copycutter.
A follower who did it to fit in.
And now I can't stop.

I bet if my IQ was even
a pimple-bump above average,
I would've thought of that
before I made the first cut.

But I didn't think.
About anything.
Except—

my perpetually perfect sister
my Judge Judy mother
my Piglet father
my no-sprinkles future
my incurable case of Ordinary
the sting of being alone
and the rush of being accepted.

On second thought,
maybe it's the little problems
that pile up the worst.

Deeper and darker.
One after another.

Until there's no light at all.

But at Least I'm Not an Idiot

Like Tara who #cut4sid.

That all started because some troll
tweeted about how Sid Riff
was smoking pot instead of
recording albums like a hottie should,
and some fans decided to cut themselves
and post pictures to show Sid how sad they were
that he was turning into a bad person
and making their whole lives a lie.

24 hours
30,000 messages
and 23 million impressions later,

Tara came to school with the words
cut4sid carved into her thigh
and a smile as wide as Texas
because she'd been retweeted
4,962 times.

It was the highlight of her year.

And the funny thing is,
she doesn't even like Sid Riff.

But that's the kind of thing
competitive cutters do.

And that's exactly what my mother
would never understand.
How cutting's everywhere now.
On a whole new level.
Not just in the closet.
Sometimes people do it because
of their deep, dark secrets,
or to fit in with friends,
or to piss off parents,
or to be razor rock stars.

But who cares why we do it.
It's a stupid question.
So when my mother asks,
I don't even answer.

By the Time My Mother Leaves

The urge to cut is so strong
it feels like Saran Wrap around my brain.
No other thoughts getting in or out.

If I was at home right now
I'd bolt up the stairs,
three at a time,
not looking back,
until I got to the bathroom,
where I'd lock the door,
turn on the shower,
hover over the sink and
slice,

    slice,

        slice.
God I miss that feeling!

The rush.
The calm.
The way the blood pools warm at first
then cools like morning dew on slivered skin.

The sway.
The swirl.

The way the crimson dances 'round the bowl
then trickles tiny teardrops down the drain.

The crimp.
The curl.
The sound Saran Wrap makes as it unsticks
and finally lets the air back to my brain.

Skylar Notices Me

"Try this instead," she says.

And then she shows me how to snap
a rubber band against my wrist.
It's not as good as cutting.
But somehow the steady rubber sting
settles down my nerves enough for me to draw.

I look at my limp, leaking girl
lying worthless on the paper.
She deserves hands, I think.

To wave hello.
To catch bouquets.
To squeeze palm to palm.

Not hands to hold a blade.

But I can't seem to draw them right.
They're lifeless, unnatural, cold.
They make me want to tear the paper up.

So I sketch the moon instead.
Moons are easy.

A white, unblinking eye
watching through the window.
Like a god who sees bad things
happening to good people every day
but doesn't even care.

Skylar glances at my drawing.
She's writing a poem,
counting syllables on her fingers
one by one.

Skylar thinks God *does* care.
Even when it doesn't feel like it.
And she's pretty sure that one day
God will lift all the pain right off her
and toss it aside like an old jacket.

But for now, she's wearing it tight.
Zipped up to the chin.
Just like me.

Skylar Shows Me Her Poem

Silent sobbing. No one sees.
Weeping like the willow trees.
Feel my heart about to pop.
Need to make the aching stop.
See moon's shimmer softly pass.
On the shards of broken glass.

It's an ekphrastic poem.
That's what Skylar calls it.
She says that means the poem
was inspired by a piece of artwork.

My artwork.

I tell her that *ekphrastic*
is the dumbest word I've ever heard.
It doesn't sound very poetic to me.
More like a hairball that the cat coughed up.

But *her* words are poetic.

Beautiful.
    Powerful.
        Painful.

Like she cut out a piece of herself
and left it lying there on the paper,
just so I'd know—

I'm
not
alone.

Jag Is Sitting on the Windowsill Nearby

He's staring at the moon.

Thousands of miles from here.

I wonder if he's thinking about
the three goals he wrote for Roger's exercise:

     x   Get out of here without the family meeting.
     x   Get out of here without the family meeting.
     x   Get out of here without the family meeting.

But the sad thing is nobody gets out
of here without that almighty meeting.
Especially when decking your dad
is what got you here in the first place.

Donya's Staring at the Moon Too

But she doesn't call it the moon.
She calls it *Lunabella*
because that sounds like
a sexy-hot girl who would
meet her at Chicory's
and drink café mochas
until they were both
as happy as exclamation points,
and they'd hold hands
on top of the table
not just underneath
even when Donya's
stupid parental unit
steamed in
hotter than coffee
ranting about how two girls
holding hands was a sin.

I ask Donya if that really happened.

But she doesn't answer.

Instead she just says that Skylar
can tell her so-called God

to shove His so-called plans
and stop messing up
every minute of
her so-called *life*!

Jag Hops off the Windowsill

"My father's Higher Power was a lightbulb," he says.
"A 60-watt incandescent."

Jag tells us how he used to go to Al-Anon meetings
before his father drank up all their savings
and started talking with his fists.

"AA lets you believe God can be anything or anyone," he says.
"Like God can be Buddha or a ceiling tile or even a lightbulb.
It doesn't really matter. As long as you believe that *something*
is your Higher Power."

I ask Jag if AA would let Colin Krusher be God.

"I know Colin is more like a fallen TV angel," I say.
"But he's been resurrected four times on my favorite show
and he's the only angel who's lasted through series nine
so that pretty much makes him immortal, if you ask me.
Plus, in real life, Colin founded a charity that gives away
shoes and umbrellas and mattresses to old people
who haven't had a new bed in like half a century.
So Colin deserves to be God way more than a 60-watt."

Jag nods and looks at the floor.

"Yeah. I guess Colin could be God," he says.
"But just so you know,
that lightbulb thing
didn't turn out too good for my dad."

Lights Out

Donya's grinding her teeth again.
Like she's mad at half the world.

I bet my dad doesn't have to
listen to a racket like this
when he's at the Hyatt
or the Holiday Inn
a thousand miles
away from home.

I bet he props himself up
on fluffy hypoallergenic pillows
and drinks four-dollar bottled waters
and watches the 10-p.m. news
with all the comings and goings
of some random city.

And even though he'll only
stay there a day, maybe two,
I bet Dad cares more
about what's happening
in De Kalb, Illinois,
or Madison, Wisconsin,
than he cares about

what's happening
to me.

My ~~Dream~~ on the Second Night

I'm on that dark country road again,
where the sky is purple
and the air is so full of static
the hairs rise up on my arms.

Then I see that horse.
The gruesome, white, wild-eyed horse.
Flaring her nostrils.
Rearing her head.
Like a warning.

I want to bolt back into consciousness.
But right away I can tell
it's one of those hosed dreams
where you can't wake yourself up
no matter how hard you try.

I'm trapped.
Immobile.
Suffocating.

But then I hear Rennie's voice:

Just one cut and you can breathe.

When she appears,
she's ten feet tall.
On freaky spider legs
just like the ones in Dalí's paintings.
And I figure that right about now
Dalí would probably drop the spoon,
wake himself up,
and paint some freaky clocks.

But I'm stuck watching Rennie
as she mounts the horse
and wraps her legs around its belly.
When she grabs its mane, the horse bucks and flails,
and I feel my heart thud like a nine-pound hammer.

Thump-thump.
Thump-thump.
Thump-thump.

Then the horse begins to run.
A great Goliath gallop
that shakes the ground
and spits mud in every direction.
I know what's coming next,
even before the white flesh
tears across the barbs.

I hear a voice screaming in my head:

Wake up.
Wake up.
Just drop the freaking spoon already!

Then the dream ends.
Just like that.
I'm sitting on the edge of my bed.
Catching my breath.
Feeling as psycho as Dalí.

Dreams Are Just a Body's Way of Sorting Things Out

That's what Ding Dong says.

I sit at the night-nurse station
while she rifles through my chart
checking to see if Mom authorized
any medication like sleeping pills.

Fat chance of that.

But I let Ding Dong search anyway,
digging through random papers,
jabbering away.

"Did you have one of them falling-down dreams?
Then you're probably just feeling helpless. That's all.
Or maybe you dreamed about being naked.
Was that it? You don't have to hide it, girl.
That doesn't mean nothing bad. You're just shy."

She pauses and stares at me hard.
Then shivers shimmy across her shoulders.

"I think you had one of them ugly dreams.
Where your teeth were falling out."

That one makes me smile
and I think about telling her
I had a whole set of snaggleteeth
that wiggled like worms
right out of my mouth,
because that kind of dream
might get her dreads in a wad,
and then maybe she'd give me the meds
without my mother's precious signature.

But I don't say a word.

Because I'm afraid if I open my mouth
the white horse might gallop out instead.
So I go back to bed pill-less and prickly,
all twisted up by the last thing she said:

"Trust me, girl. Whatever it was,
that dream is tellin' you something."

Thursday 7:16 a.m.

Breakfast on the second day.

I see a butterfly on Skylar's arm,
a swallowtail with swooping swirls
and polka-dot wings.

She drew it herself with a black Sharpie.

"For the Butterfly Project," she says.

Then she tells me how it works.

First, you feel the urge to cut,
but instead of picking up the blade
you pick up a pen
and draw a butterfly
on your arm
or your ankle
or anywhere you want.
It doesn't really matter
as long as it's on your body.

Then you name it for someone special.
That's what brings the butterfly to life.

So now you've got this living, breathing ink
on your forearm or by your belly button
or the dimple behind your knee,
and the butterfly is flapping its wonderful wings
while you take algebra tests and clean your room
and eat cold chicken nuggets in the cafeteria.
And because you love it so much
you stay away from the blade
because that's the only way
to save your swallowtail's life.

You can't wash it off either.
The butterfly has to fade on its own.
Because if you wash it off in the sink
or cut before the ink fades naturally,
then your butterfly dies.

Those are the rules.

Sick, huh?

But Skylar's so sure it'll work,
she floats away from the table
like she's a butterfly herself.

I don't know if I should feel
sorry for her

for putting so much faith
in permanent marker
or if I should feel
just a teeny bit good inside
because Skylar named her butterfly

for me.

Skylar's Nervous Breakdown

It's all Bullhorn's fault.
She never should've said that
Skylar's gonna become another
Teenage Statistic if she doesn't
start seeing herself for
the Beautiful Person that she is.

Then Donya wouldn't have said,
"Oh yeah, twigs are soooo hot."

And Jag wouldn't have laughed
until chocolate milk spurted out his nose.

And Skylar wouldn't have bolted
down the hallway screaming,
"Lemmeout! Lemmeout!"

And I wouldn't have sat there
with my mouth open
wishing I'd said thank you
for the butterfly.

There's So Much Drama

My mother thinks it's all because
of the hormones in cow's milk
making girls hit puberty way too soon.
And not just the early bloomers.
A whole generation of twelve-year-olds
budding in their teeny-weeny bikinis
and sprouting armpit hair
before their frontal lobes
have a chance to catch up.

But what does she know?

My mother also thinks that margarine
is one molecule away from plastic
and that fried food will make
her hair turn gray.

That's whacked.

But sometimes I wish she was right,
because to tell you the truth,
I'd give up dairy products altogether
if it would make all the drama go away.

And Skylar come back.

Before Group Therapy

I'm staring at Jag's
perfect pecs,
his awesome abs,
his flawless face,
when Roger points
at sneakers propped
on Skylar's empty seat
and says,

"Take them off."

And then . . .

Plop.
        Plop.

I'm staring at Jag's
pissed and perfect feet.

The Three C's of Addiction

Why does Roger look at me like that?

I've never soaked gummy bears in vodka
or snuck off campus to get high at lunch,
and just because I smoked pot
one time with Rennie,
that doesn't mean
I'm addicted.

But Roger says
if you *crave* something
and lose *control*
and keep doing it
over and over
despite the *consequences*,
then you're addicted.

Yeah?
So what?
Why does he keep looking at me like that?

What I Find in Skylar's ~~Empty~~ Room

Five carrot sticks she pretended to eat at lunch.

Four clumps of hair that brushed right off her head.

Three unopened letters.

Two bloody tissues.

And a poem she wrote today—

What the ~~Blade~~ Says

I am the shadow
that waits in dark places,
silent and patient,
to follow you home.

I am the tiger
that eagerly chases,
racing and running,
wherever you roam.

I am the hunger
that feeds on your madness,

biting and clawing,
to swallow you whole.

I am the silver
that soaks up your sadness,
body and spirit
and all of your soul.

The Rubber Room

Donya finds me in Skylar's room
and sees the bloody tissues in the trash.
She says she knows exactly what that
means and she pulls me out of the room.
She points down this long narrow hall,
past the rec room and the emergency exit,
to a thick black door with a tiny slit of a window.

I tell Donya we shouldn't go,
not because the room is *restricted*
but because if Skylar *is* in there
I don't want to see her,
not like that.

But Donya makes me go.

Well, not exactly *makes* me.
I mean, it's not like she drags
me by the hair. But she has this way
of making you think that *not* doing
something is way worse than doing it,
no matter how bad that something seems.

Sort of like Rennie.

So we slip past Bullhorn
on our rubber-soled socks
and we figure we've got like
two and a half minutes until
Bullhorn discovers that we're gone.
But even before we get to the door
I hear this sound that makes me
want to turn around again.

I wouldn't call it crying exactly.
It's more high-pitched than that,
like a kitten.

Donya pushes me to the window.
This time with more than her words.

"Is she in there?"

The window is smudged and the room gray,
so I can't make anything out at first,
except for how the walls look like
they're covered in mattresses,
and the floor is sort of spongy.

But then I see something
in the far back corner,

and I feel my ears get hot
like they always do when I'm mad.

"Is it her?"

"See for yourself," I say.

Then I brush past Donya
pissed at her for making me look,
because that's the kind of picture
I'll never get out of my head.

That poor little pencil stabber.

He looks so much like Sean.

I Need to Chill

So I wedge myself by the window and I watch
garbagemen heaving green plastic cans,
and a man running to catch the bus,
and a woman walking her mop dog
and wrapping up its poop like a present.

It's like there are two worlds now.

The In Here.
And the Out There.

The suspended animation.
And the full speed ahead.

And suddenly I'm desperate
to know what Rennie's doing.

In the Out There.

Right now.

This very minute.

My One Phone Call

It feels like a century since I saw Rennie
through that dirty squad-car window,
looking sort of shocked and mad,
like someone had splashed water in her face.
She must've been really pissed at the cop.

I drum my fingers on the counter
as the phone rings five times.

Come on. Come on.
I know you're in art class.
Just pick up already.

And then I hear her.

"This better be good."

Her words are like punches
knocking the breath out of me.
I want her to say:

OMG! Are you okay?
This is sooooo unfair!

Are they gonna let you out soon?
Everybody misses you like crazy.

But something's off.

"I just wanted to talk," I say.

"So talk," she answers.

I hear water running and someone giggling
in the background. Then Rennie sighs,
like she's bored with me already.

"Look. The school's on high alert," she says.
"A message went home telling parents to be
on guard for the Top Ten Signs of Self-Harm
and now every mom in Manatee County
is searching for scissors under the bed
and taking inventory of their Band-Aid boxes."

I hear the phone changing hands
and another voice jumps on the line.

"You can't even get a plastic knife
in the cafeteria thanks to you."

And right away I'm sick to my stomach because I know who it is. That growly, annoying, gag-me voice could only be coming from one person.

And that's Tara.

Yeah.

The Two-Face.

Shower Escape

All I want is scalding water
to sear down my spine
like a hot blade,
to blister my back,
to char my chest,
to melt me to pieces
so I can dissolve down the drain,
evaporate into steam,
and disappear.

That would feel good right now.
That would make sense.

But all I can find is one button,
no hot or cold knob,
no temperature dial,
just a single silver square
that says On/Off
like a light switch,
and when I press it
the drops that spill
like lukewarm milk
aren't even as hot as my tears.

I feel my lips start to quiver,
and my shoulders shake.
Then my heart splits open
and the words tumble out
like bricks.

"How could Rennie say that?
I thought she was my friend.
My sister."

But nobody answers.
Not even my own echo.
The shower shuts off automatically,
and I'm still sobbing, watching
ribbons of water slide down my skin.
The drops glance over the scars on my hips,
and ricochet past the cuts on my thighs,
and bounce off the red flippy lines on my ankles
like balls in a pinball machine.

I'm an outcast,
      a loser,
            a nothing.

I step out of the shower and drag
the towel across my body, but

I can't look at myself anymore,
because every inch of rejected skin
reminds me of the awful truth:

Now I have more scars than friends.

All I Want to Do

Is sleep and sleep and
sleepandsleepandsleepand
sleepandsleepandsleepand
sleepandsleepandsleepand
sleepandsleepandsleepand
sleepandsleepandsleepand
sleepandsleepandsleepand
sleepandsleepandsleepand
sleepandsleepandsleepand
sleepandsleepandsleep . . .

But I'm the kind of tired
that sleeping doesn't fix.

Ten Things Rennie Never Told Me

That cuts multiply like freaking rabbits.

That no skin is sacred.

That hugs hurt.

That becoming a pathological liar is a requirement.

That guilt feels like being buried alive.

That long sleeves ride up at the worst possible moment.

That being called *emo* sucks.

That cutting can get you Baker Acted in Florida.

That people are disposable.

And that one day, she'd get rid of *me*.

Bullhorn Brings a Tray to My Room

She tells me I need to eat.
Then she stands there waiting,
like applesauce will solve everything.

I stare at the ham sandwich cut diagonally.
The sticks of marbled string cheese.
The bunch of green grapes.

For a split second I flash back
to when I was four years old,
watching Mom peel grapes
one by one
so I won't choke on the skin.

Mom laughs as they slip through her fingers
and says she doesn't know why she's
still peeling them. I'm not a baby anymore.
But she keeps doing it anyway,
grape after grape,
because that's the way I like them.

Then for the first time in forever,
I get that cookie-dough feeling.
The warm, out-of-the-oven emotion
that a little girl can only feel for her mother.

And I wonder what snuffed that feeling out.

If it was Avery with her
I'm-the-favorite-daughter routine.

Or if it was Rennie with her relentless
mother bashing—like:
Don't-expect-a-thank-you-just-
for-pushing-me-out-of-your-vagina.

Or if maybe
    somehow
        it was me.

Because I believed them both.

As If Things Weren't ~~Bad~~ Enough

The Pomeranian shows up with her clipboard.
I don't know if I have the strength
to fake my way through her questions today.

Plus I'd really rather see why there's such
a commotion in the lobby behind her,
but I can't make it out because she's filling
the whole doorframe with her polyester suit.

While I'm craning my neck, she reads
from the same stupid script as yesterday:

1. Do you know why you're here?
    Apparently, so Rennie can dump me for the Two-Face.

2. Do you think you need to be here?
    It doesn't matter where I am. The whole world sucks.

3. What would you do if we let you out?
    I'll give you one guess.

Of course, I don't say what I'm thinking.

That's the thing about lies.
Once you get good at them,

they feel more natural than the truth,
almost as automatic as breathing,
and sometimes when I'm feeling
low and lost like now,
I can't even tell the difference.

Some Friend I Am

It was Skylar in the lobby
making all that commotion,
because she came back
with fresh gauze on her arm
and two curvy, red lines
bleeding through the cloth like smiles.

Here's the problem with that.

It's not that I think any less of her
even though my heart cringes a little
because I know she wanted to stay clean.

It's not that the butterfly's dead
even though she named it for me
and thinking of myself as a dead insect
sort of sucks.

It's not even that I'm worried
about what'll happen to Skylar next
even though the Pomeranian
is talking to her waaaay too long.

The problem is this:

I can't *be there* for her
even though I want to,
because those two tiny lines
are a huge freaking trigger
and they're making me
double over and sweat
until all I can think about
is ripping apart my own cuts
with my shaky bare hands.

How screwed up is that?

~~I Hate~~ It When People Say

If cutting's so bad, you should just quit.

Yeah, right.

Like I can snap my fingers
and make my blades disappear.
They have absolutely no idea
how freaking hard it is to stop.

Why don't you just quit breathing?

That's what I want to say.

Let's see how that works out for you.

Roger Must Have Some Kind of Radar

Because he taps me on the shoulder and leads
me to his office, which is barely big enough
for a goldfish, by the way.

I'm still feeling triggered and edgy,
and I expect him to say a bunch of
touchy-feely crap like:

Tell me what you're feeling now.
Or
Does Skylar's arm make you upset?
Or
What kind of memories does this bring up for you?

The last thing I expect is for him to lean over,
open his desk drawer and pull out a jelly jar.
But that's exactly what he does.
Only there isn't jelly in it anymore.
It's filled with water and glitter,
kind of like a snow globe
but way more beautiful,
because the flecks are thick and gold
and mesmerizing in the weirdest way.

Roger calls it a *calming jar.*

He gives it a little shake and hands it to me,
and while I'm watching the liquid swirl
and the glitter blink like a billion stars,
the strangest thing starts to happen.

I feel my breathing steady and my pulse slow down
and a trail of goose bumps tiptoe up my arms,
just like when I was little and Mom traced letters
on my back with her finger.

I wish I could take the jar to my room and shake it
for like the next 26 hours until I get out of here.
But there's no chance of that, on account of the glass.
So I watch it for as long as I can in Roger's office,
until the blanket of gold folds on itself one last time,
and the glitter settles to the bottom like stardust.

Roger tells me he'll give me the recipe,
to make a calming jar of my own at home,
because sometimes, he says, all you need is a distraction.

Things to Do Instead of Cutting

Roger wants to use afternoon group
for a mega-brainstorming session.
We're gonna go through everyone's problems.
Starting with cutting.

He comes up with a few ideas himself
and writes them on the whiteboard
with a squeaky purple pen.

GO FOR A WALK.
TAKE A BUBBLE BATH.
TALK TO SOMEONE WHO CARES.

I don't know what makes me do it.
Maybe I feel sort of bad for Roger
standing up there all alone
with those big, expectant eyes
that nobody will look at.
Or maybe I feel like I owe him
for showing me that glitter jar.
Either way, I decide to give in.

"Draw something," I say.

Roger's face lights up and he pens
my answer in swoopy grape letters.
And then it's sort of contagious
because everyone stops
sitting on their hands,
and counting ceiling tiles,
and pretending to be asleep,
and they start giving up ideas faster
than Roger can write them down,
starting with Jag:

"Punch a pillow.
Jump on your bed.
Scream at the sky."

And, yeah, I know that sounds like
Jag has anger-management issues,
but just like Roger says,
there's no wrong answers here,
so don't get any bad ideas about Jag.
And besides, I could think about that
sexy skater boy jumping on his bed
in baggy white boxers all day long!
Of course Donya has to try to outdo him:

"Throw fruit off your roof.
Stand on your head.
Dye your hair."

And I have to bite my tongue
to stop myself from saying
that she doesn't have enough hair
on that weed-wacked Mohawk of hers
to bother with any more dye.
But that's just because I'm jealous
her ideas were better than mine.

But the one who blows us all away is Skylar.
And not just with her rubber-band fix
or the butterfly project. She's got a whole
truckload of suggestions that she rattles off
effortlessly, like she's tried every one:

"Eat chocolate.
Hug a puppy.
Read John Green.

"Make jewelry.
Join a fandom.
Write a poem.

"Blow bubbles.
Play piano.
Sing 'Who Says.'

"Watch *Juno*.
Order pizza.
Clean your room.

"Surf Tumblr.
Do your homework.
Say a prayer."

Roger has to stop writing there because
he runs out of room on the whiteboard,
which kind of stinks because he doesn't
get down some of Skylar's funniest ideas, like:

Watch English YouTubers,
then talk with a British accent all day,

or

Rub peppermint oil all over your body,

or

Put glue on your hands and then peel it off later.

By the time the afternoon session is over,
we're all joking and laughing
and it feels so good for a change
that nobody even mentions
how Skylar came up with like
937 Things to Do Instead of Cutting,
but she's the one who's sitting here
with a brand-new bandage on her arm.

How Did You Do It?

I know I shouldn't ask.
But not asking feels like being
on a diet and having a big bowl
of chocolate ice cream shoved in front of me.

Like what am I supposed to do?
Just sit here and watch it melt?

Besides, Skylar doesn't mind.
I think she *wants* to tell me.
After all, it was *my* butterfly she killed.

"I took the Scotch tape off the nurse's desk
when that little boy came in. Remember?
Nobody was paying any attention."

I think about that sweet serrated edge
and that hot, hard tape dispenser
and I have to shake the image
from my mind because picturing
those plastic teeth biting into my skin
is making pins and needles dance on
all my favorite places.

"It's an addiction, you know," Skylar says.
"Just like drugs or alcohol."

I try to shake her off, but she keeps going.

"Endorphins are like narcotics.
That's why we crave them so bad.
I'm not saying that's the only reason we cut.
There's like a million scars out there
and each one has its own story.

"But every cutter would agree with me on this—
Once you start, it's really hard to quit."

Skylar tells me she had a long talk about it
with Dr. McKay, and it takes me a minute
to realize she means the Pomeranian.

"I'm really sorry about the butterfly," she adds.
"But Dr. McKay says I've taken a HUGE first step.
Just by admitting I have a problem. So maybe,
in a way, your butterfly saved me."

She bites her lower lip and fidgets in her seat
like she's trying hard to believe her own words.
But somehow she's not sure. Then she pulls my

arm into her lap, and before I can yank it away
she swirls her black Sharpie across my wrist.

"Your first butterfly!"

She smiles and says how it's stronger because she
drew it for me, instead of me drawing it for myself.
Then she adds a dot to each antenna and tells me
I need to name it. And it's just like when someone
sets out a birthday cake and says,

"Blow out the candles and make a wish."

You can't really help yourself.
The wish just pops into your head,
and before you know it, people are clapping,
and wax is dripping all over the frosting.

That's how it is with Sean's name.
It just pops into my head.
Like a wish.

A wish to be a better big sister.

A wish to be a halfway decent role model.

And most of all, a wish not to be
a pathological liar who someday cuts herself
with her little brother's Cub Scout knife
and traumatizes him so bad that
he ends up locked in a rubber room
just like that poor pencil stabber.

Thing to Do #826

I don't know why, but even after
Skylar draws the butterfly on me,
I'm still thinking about that plastic
tape dispenser and I decide to start
talking with an English accent.
Just like Dan and Phil.
From YouTube.

"Hello, Love," I say.
"Have you seen Dan and Phil?
Well, they're bloody brilliant!
I just saw their shoot on Pancake Day,
and Dan wore his trousers 'round his arse."

Skylar joins in with her pinky in the air
like she's sipping Earl Grey and she says
how she'd fancy another cup.

And Donya says, "Get off your bum,
you lazy wanker, and get the tea yourself."

Then Jag tells Donya to piss off.
But not in a mean way.
More as a joke.

And we talk about how
Attaboys smells like a loo
and therapy sessions are rubbish
and we can't wait to get our own flats
so we can faff around all day
and do nothing but watch BBC on the telly.

It's fun talking like this.
Oh bloody hell.
It's aces.

And it makes me forget
about the tape dispenser.

Completely.

Ding Dong Tells Me—No Visitors Today

But that's okay.

Because Mom's picking Dad up at the airport,
so he'll be here for tomorrow's family meeting.
And I suppose there was only one flight available
from O'Hare to TIA and that was the 6 p.m.

The exact same time as visiting hour.

And I guess there must've been no taxicabs,
or airport shuttles, or rental cars, or buses
in the entire state of Florida, so the only option
was for Mom to circle around the terminal
in her Lexus until Dad's plane touched down.

That's the reason they're not here.

It's not because Mom thinks her car's gonna
get jacked in this *lovely* part of town,

or because Avery needs a ride to gymnastics,

or because Dad can't look at me yet.

It's just a transportation problem.

Small Talk

Since we don't have any visitors,
Ding Dong lets me and Jag watch TV,
but I have to sit on the end of the couch
and Jag has to straddle the beanbag chair
and she makes us promise to keep an invisible
hula hoop of space between us at all times.

"I'm watchin' you, my little bandulus,"
Ding Dong says as she walks out.

But she has nothing to worry about,
because as soon as I'm alone with Jag,
I feel like I'm in one of those space-saving
storage bags with every ounce of air sucked
out and my thoughts are winter sweaters,
stuck together, flat as pancakes.

It's a good thing Jag likes to talk.

He skates over every inch of awkward silence
telling me how he kickflips and ollies and caspers
as good as Tony Hawk. And even though I'd trip
just looking at a skateboard, Jag makes me feel like
I'm right there with him, sliding and grinding down
ledges and rails.

"It's dangerous," he says. "That's why I like it."

Then he raises his shirt and shows me a patch
of road rash chaffed across his ribs. But when he
sees my eyes wander to the small red-brown circles
singed on his side, he covers up again.

"They're old," he says. "Cigarette burns."

He wrings his hands and looks at the clock,
and I can tell he thinks I'm judging him,
like self-harm is some kind of girl problem,
and any boy who would snuff out cigs on his
own skin must be weak or wimpy or worse.

Every brain cell in my head is screaming out
how wrong he is, that I don't think that at all,
but I'm stuck in the vacuum bag without an
ounce of oxygen and it takes everything I have
just to squeak out two tiny words.

"It's okay," I say.

The room is dead still. And I'm worried that
I hurt him without even meaning to.

But then Jag smiles and runs his hand
through his hair and starts telling me about
this electric blue RipStik he's gonna
buy when he gets out of here.
And I feel this huge rush of relief.

I guess sometimes
two words
are just enough.

Skylar's Being Transferred

Yeah.
Right now.
At 6:30 p.m.

When I should be pulling her aside
and telling her about my amazing,
wordless conversation with Jag.
But she has to go.
Just like that.

They're taking her to a long-term
treatment center because Attaboys
doesn't actually *treat* anybody.
Unless you count the drive-by pep talks
and a few minutes with a jelly jar.

They're just a stabilization facility,
kind of like a drunk tank for psychos,
where they wait to see if you sober up
and get your head on straight.

But if you don't stabilize,
if you're still a danger to self or others,
if you decide to rip your arm up

with a tape dispenser,
well then that's it,
you're gonna get committed to a place
where there's even more chicken wire
in the window glass than here.

Before she leaves,
Skylar says good-bye
to everybody one by one,
and she saves me for last.

"I'm sorry you have to go," I say.

"I need to," she answers. "So I can get better."

And this time she seems sure of it.

I think about her telling me how killing
my butterfly might've saved her and
how admitting that she was addicted
felt like a *huge* first step.

I still can't believe she told
the Pomeranian of all people.
But Skylar insists it was
the right thing to do.

"It feels like such a weight off," she says.

She rests her cheek on my shoulder
and gives me an armless hug,
so we don't hurt each other.

Then she slips me a piece of paper.

"I even wrote it down.
So I'd never forget how bad it got.
It's kind of like a confession."

When Skylar walks out,
she's smiling and waving,
tracing infinity signs in the air
with a feathery finger.

Friends forever.

I want to run after her
and get her phone number
even though that's against the rules.
But before I can move my feet
or swallow the lump in my throat,
the double doors shut and Skylar's gone.

Just like that robin in the sky.

Skylar's Confession

I wait a long time before I open it,
maybe because I'm afraid that
Skylar's words will be like a mirror.
I might see myself in them.

When I unfold the paper,
I feel my chest tighten up
like a charley horse in my heart,
but I can't stop thinking about
how Skylar looked when she left,
with her wide smile and her
infinitely happy hands.

So I force myself to read the poem
because I want to see how heavy
this weight must've been. How
getting it off her chest could make
her float like a feather.

And I just gotta say,
it was pretty freaking heavy.

This is what she wrote:

I made the first cut razor thin,
a gentle kiss on virgin skin,

then traded nights of peaceful sleep
for kisses that grew dark and deep,

until the slices on my thighs
soon withered hearts of butterflies,

and now there's nothing left but this—
my aching for that empty kiss.

There's a ~~Battle~~ Going On inside My Head

On one side there's Skylar,
putting the mirror in my hand,
telling me to take a real good look at myself.

On the other side there's Rennie
and all the Sisters of the Broken Glass,
breaking the mirror and handing me the sharpest piece.

And Skylar is saying:

Stay strong.
Keep fighting.
Just admit you need help.

But Rennie is saying:

Have fun.
Feel good.
There's nothing to admit.

And even though Skylar's a two-ounce Tweety Bird
and Rennie's a ten-foot, spider-legged giant,
they start to go at it, beak against claws,
and there's no telling who's gonna win.

Before Bed, I Make Two Lists

I figure the first list is going to be the longest
since that's where I'm writing all the facts
that prove I'm not really addicted to cutting.

The second list is supposed to be short.
With the one or two things I hate about it.
Like the lying part.
And the laundry stains.

But that's not exactly how it turns out.

Five Facts that Prove I'm Not ~~Addicted~~

1. I don't do it every day.

2. I can stop at just one cut.

3. I've never tried crazy places like my feet.

4. I don't go very deep.

5. I quit once. For the whole summer!

Five Reasons That's Total Bullshit

It's all I think about.
It's all I think about.
It's all I think about.
It's all I think about.

Even in my dreams.

First Prayer in Forever

I can't sleep thinking about those
stupid lists and I'm getting sick
of counting cracks in the wall.
So I start thinking about what
Jag said the other day.

How God could be whoever
I understand Him to be.

That doesn't seem as pushy as I
remembered from my old church
with those stiff wooden pews
and all that Our Father and Kingdom Come crap.

It seems sorta . . . I don't know . . . inviting.

So I figure, what the hell. Maybe I should pray.
What's the worst that could happen?
Who knows? It might even put me to sleep.

So I do that sign of the cross thing.
Backward probably. Then I close my eyes
and sort of talk in my head. Like

Hey God.

It's Kenna.

Remember me?

I'm stuck here
in this psycho ward.

But you already know that.

Anyway . . .

You're probably pissed at me
for the whole cutting thing
because of the Bible business
that says how my body's supposed
to be a temple and all.

But I don't feel like a temple.
I feel like a shack.

And here's the thing—

Once I get out of here,
there's gonna be triggers
around every corner,
and blades in my purse,
and voices in my head
telling me to use them.

And I'm sorry to say this,
but I probably will.
That's just the way it is.
I don't feel like I have a choice,
or another road to take, or whatever.

And don't worry.
I don't expect you to fix me.

But I was sort of thinking maybe
you could do some of that God stuff,
with your hands on my head or whatever,
and just make the pain a little looser,
so it doesn't always feel like a jacket
wrapped around me so tight.

And maybe you could do that for Skylar, too.

That would be good.

Then I try to remember how
prayers are supposed to end,
with *lay me down to sleep,*
and souls to keep, and all that
other nursery rhyme stuff,
but that doesn't seem to fit.
So finally, I just say *Thanks, God,*

and I roll over on my pillow.

Then the strangest thing happens.

I don't see angels or hear harps
or feel the hand of God
slipping into my life
just when I need him.

The lightbulb doesn't flicker
and Colin Krusher doesn't materialize
through the air duct (*dammit*).

It's nothing like that.
It's way more subtle.
And I'm sure some people
would say it's all in my head.
But all I can say is that it *does* feel
like my troubles are looser somehow,
like the jacket isn't zipped
to my chin anymore.
And it's not like I jump
up and down on the bed yelling,
Holy crap!
It worked.
But I say it to myself.

Real quiet.

My Dream on the Third Night

So take a guess where I am.
Dark country road.
Electric purple sky.
Yada yada yada.

And here comes that freaking white horse.

Only this time, she's sort of still.
Like she's thinking about something.

And I'm calm too, scanning the road.
Waiting for somebody.
And I know they're coming
because I feel so inflated,
it's like I'm walking on helium.

Then Jag rolls up on his RipStik,
and I can tell right away
he's the one I've been waiting for,
because my heart floats even higher
and we seem to talk without words.

He sees a patch of flowers by the road,
white fairy orchids growing wild,

and he smiles that crooked smile
and leans to pick one for me.

And then, here's where the dream goes to shit.

When Jag stands back up,
there's a sea of spiders at his feet,
so many spiders that it looks like
the ground is moving.

And in fact, the ground *is* moving.
It's opening up like the mouth of a sinkhole
and Jag is losing his footing and spiraling in,
and the last thing I see before it swallows him up,
are the five pointed petals of white fairy orchid
spilling to the ground like falling stars.

The horse is going ballistic now.
She's bucking and snorting and
making all kinds of terrible sounds
that should never come out of an animal.

She rears away from the fence again and again,
but in the end she tears her flesh across the barbs.

I run to her and throw my arms around her neck.
I try to stop the bleeding, but the harder I squeeze,
the more the blood flows. It's like a stream spilling
down the horse's shoulders, splashing to the earth.
I pull off my jacket and press the cloth against her skin.
I can hear her heavy breath and feel her deep, dark pulse
throbbing beneath my fingers. Like we're connected.

Thump-thump.
Thump-thump.
Thump-thump.

Then I feel something shift.

And suddenly I'm not holding the horse anymore.

I look down only to discover that I'm
pressing the jacket against my own arm,
feeling the beat of my own pulse,
watching the cloth turn red,
under the light of the moon.

I Wake Up

So that's it?
That's what the dream means?
I'm the freaking horse?

I storm out of the bedroom and
head straight to Ding Dong's desk.

"Did you dream about them teeth again?" she asks.

I shake my head and start ranting.
This time I don't hold anything back.
Not one single detail.

I figure Ding Dong's going to make a big deal
about all the dark images like the black sky
and lightning and how that probably means
I'm on some kind of evil path. Or maybe
she's gonna key in on Rennie and the spiders
and say that means I'm caught in a web.

But Ding Dong doesn't seem to care
about any of that. All she wants to know
is what the horse is doing.

The bucking.
The kicking.
The flailing.
The fury.

Ding Dong takes it all in, studying me with her dark eyes,
and I wait for her big dream interpretation to ramble out.
But in the end, she has only one thing to say:

"Seems to me, if you are that horse,
you're tryin' awfully hard to fight that fence."

And that's all I can think about for the rest of the night.

Friday 8 a.m.

Donya's packing up.

Her 72 hours were officially over last night,
but her mom works second shift at a factory,
soldering circuit boards, and Donya says
the supervisor's a real prick and wouldn't
let her mom off. So she's coming today instead.

I don't ask Donya about her dad.

It feels weird.
How I know so many things about Donya,
but I don't really know anything at all.

Like I know
that when Donya's tense she grinds her teeth,
and that her hair color isn't permanent
because she leaves purple streaks in the sink,
and that there really *was* a girl at Chicory's
because Donya cries about it in her sleep.

I know all those inside-out, private little things.

But I don't even know Donya's last name
or where she lives, or goes to school,

or if that buzz-gone-wrong
was really something more.

And I still don't know what to expect from her.
Not from one minute to the next.
Which is why I'm only half surprised
when she takes the silver stud out of her tongue.

"Going-away present," she says.

She can tell I'm trying to puzzle it out,
so she shakes her head and fills in the blanks.

"I told those idiots it was a fresh piercing.
That I had to keep it in for medical reasons.
But really, I just needed it in case of emergency."

She unscrews the bottom of the barbell
and shows me the sharp point at the end.

"Anyway, it's yours now."

She drops the stud in my hand and
I curl my fingers around it fast.
When I hear footsteps in the hall
I slip it into my pocket, like instinct.

Bullhorn tells her it's time to go,
and since Donya's not the hugging kind
she gives me a quick wink and one last *hooyah*.
Then she's gone.

Jag Says He Doesn't Have Much Choice

Military school.
The Florida Sheriff Youth Ranch.
A group home for troubled teens.
Or suck it up and do the family meeting.

We're sitting in the TV room and I say how
it sucks to be fifteen because all our so-called
choices are like the consolation prizes on a
really lame game show.

Sorry you didn't win the BRAND-NEW CAR!
But here's a bag of corn chips
and a cheesy bumper sticker.

Jag's lips curl into that sexy half smile
and I feel this global warming rise up
in my body all the way from that tickly
spot in my stomach to the top of my head.
I get so nervous that I fumble my
notebook, and little wisps of paper
flutter to the ground.

Jag drops to one knee, and I swear when
he picks them up it looks like he's holding
the five pointed petals of white fairy orchid.

And that's when the universe
starts moving in slow motion.

Jag reaches across the invisible hula hoop
of space and he touches my arm. The one
that's still laced with screaming red lines.
And suddenly I'm aware how ugly it is.
But before I can pull my arm back,
Jag leans down and plants his lips,
soft and tender,
right on my scars.

"You're beautiful," he says. "All of you."

And then this planetary blackout happens.

Or maybe I just close my eyes.
All I know is that when I open them,
Jag's already back in the beanbag chair
and Roger is walking in the door and
it almost seems like nothing happened.

Except for the blush on Jag's cheeks
and this feeling inside me
that something is different.

It's So Empty

With Skylar and Donya gone,
and Jag in Roger's office
"exploring his alternatives."

I'm all alone
with my daydreams,
and my unfinished drawing,
and Donya's good-bye present in my pocket.

I try to concentrate on pencil shading.
But the problem with drawing hands is that
they have just as much expression as a face.

They're emotional.
Personal.
Revealing.

You could paint the freaking *Mona Lisa*,
but if you gave her Skylar's happy hands
or Donya's fighting fists, the whole picture
would go to crap, because that's not who
Mona Lisa is.

I think about Skylar's question.

Is that you?

Two days ago I told her no.
But today, I think—
yeah, maybe it is.

And then I feel myself being pulled into the zone
where I'm not really thinking about what I'm drawing
but stuff is streaming out stroke after stroke and I'm so
wrapped up in the art there could be a jackhammer
blaring right next to me and I wouldn't even hear it.

I'm surprised when I put the pencil down.

They're the best hands I've ever drawn.

And they're not hiding inside sleeves, either,
with just the fingertips poking out,
holding the fabric tight so the cotton won't roll up.
They're out in the light. Palms open.
With soft, slender fingers and just enough
lines and creases to make them look real.

They're the kind of hands an art teacher might
hold up in front of the class and while the other kids

roll their eyes or crumple up their own papers,
the teacher keeps gushing away.

I mean look at these hands, she might say.

So full of hope.

One Hour Before

Roger likes my drawing.
It's much better than the crayon crap
hanging in his office where we meet
an hour before the family meeting.

He explains how he has to make sure
he's releasing me to a stable situation
and that I'll have a strong support network
on the outside.

I think he's gonna lecture me about not cutting
or how to use the 937 Things to Do Instead.

But he doesn't.

He talks about relapse.
How it's just a part of recovery.
That I shouldn't beat myself up if it happens to me.

I know he thinks he's helping
with his fancy Walmart diploma and all.
But I almost wish he would just shut up,
because it feels like he's giving me permission.

Like he knows it's inevitable.

I'm bound to screw up.

Five Minutes Before

Mom—
Shifting in her seat.
Checking the clock.
Clutching that ugly Vera Bradley
that cost her $118 but looks like
it's made out of pot holders.

Avery—
Texting away.
Twirling her hair.
Pretending she's not even here.

Dad—
Counting the floor tiles.
Raising his head.
Forcing a smile that looks like it hurts.

Me—
Closing my eyes.
Forgetting to breathe.
Thinking of what's in my pocket.

The Family Meeting

So don't be disappointed,
but there isn't a big blow-out
with screaming and finger pointing
and a gallon of guilty tears.

And there isn't some kind
of miraculous healing either.

Mom doesn't admit how she favors
Avery because Avery has the same
ghost-blue eyes as her dead first husband.

Avery doesn't come clean about all
the nasty things she says to me
behind closed doors.

Dad doesn't jump into a phone booth
and change from Piglet to Superman.

They just act the same way they always do,
and before long Roger is smiling and shaking hands
and giving them a bunch of papers to sign.

And that's when I start thinking about the ride home,
squished next to Avery, with her elbow in my ribs.
And I imagine Sean, craning in his seat, asking where
I've been until I bury him in an avalanche of white lies.

I wish I had the calming jar,
or a watermelon to throw off the roof,
or a baby beagle to hug.

But I don't.

The only things I have
are in my pocket.

It All Comes down to/This

I wonder how long it takes to sterilize
a silver stud with hot tap water.
I don't want to be gross or anything,
but I don't have much time before
Bullhorn checks on me in the bathroom.

Two minutes, I guess.
That's probably clean enough.

I close the unlockable door
and listen for the magnet to click
before I unzip my pants.

The hip would be easiest to hide.
Unless they make me undress.
Roger never told me what happens
after the family meeting.

What if they make me strip
and mark up another one of those
naked paper dolls and compare it
to the first one?

Like a Before and After.
Then I'd be screwed.

I should probably do it below the bikini
line since they didn't make me take off
my underwear in the ER.

That would be the perfect spot.

And it can be small, too.
I don't have to cut that much.
The family meeting was only halfway sucky,
and I just need a little calm to last the ride home.

I'm kind of worried about the stud though,
because it's not very sharp and I hate the
ripping feeling, which is why I quit using
glass and switched to Feather stainless,
but that blade's still in my cell phone,
so this will have to do.

I pinch the stud between my fingers
and draw a light test line three times,
which is part of my ritual,
don't ask me why,
and by the time I get to line three,
I feel static electricity racing through my chest
and every beat of my heart growing bigger
and more expectant, like it knows something
amazing is about to happen, and then there's this

swirl in the air like my body is separating from reality
and just as I'm about to plunge the point in—

BAM!

I hear the freaking Disney Channel playing
in Spanish on the other side of the wall.

And a little boy.

Laughing.

And it's not like some miracle connect-the-dots
where I think about the pencil stabber, and then
my brother, Sean, and then the butterfly on my arm,
and I'm so swept up by the Right-Thing-to-Do
that the silver stud floats out of my fingers,
and all my desire disappears like magic.

That's not how it works.

It takes every heaving breath in my body
to pull that point away from my skin.
And when I do, it doesn't feel
like I crushed a monster.

Or dodged a bullet.
Or did something to be proud of.

It feels like a freaking train wreck.

And I have to flush the stud down the toilet
just to make sure I don't pick it back up again.

But then I hear that laughing,
and I look at my arm
where I wrote

Sean

by the butterfly wing,
in caring big-sister cursive
and suddenly I'm overcome
with a gladness that the butterfly
is still alive on my arm
and not in butterfly heaven,
or wherever it is that dead
permanent marker goes.

And that's when I admit it.
Just in my head.
To myself.

One inaudible breath.

I need help.

And I wouldn't say it feels
like a *huge* first step.
Not in the Mount Everest way
that Skylar said it would.

But it definitely feels
like *something.*

And just for a second,
a swirl of promise
tickles up inside me.

And I feel calm.
Without the guilt.

Friday 3:22 p.m.

So here's the thing about being Released.

You get back everything—
your belt,
your shoelaces,
the perfume bottles from your purse,

your wallet,
your cell phone,
the blade behind the battery.

And they give you
brochures,
and pamphlets,
and these useless psych referrals.

And then that's it.

You open up the door and walk out.
And the world's still the same sharp
trigger as when you left it.

So that makes you wonder
what's gonna happen next.

Like was getting Baker Acted
enough of a wake-up call?

Or can a kiss really change you?

Or a butterfly make you strong?

I wonder that myself.

But like I said before, my life's
not some riveting novel that's
gonna tie up all neat at the end.

Not in 72 freaking hours.

The only thing I can say is that
when I walk out those doors,

I see Sean's face shining
like that blue jellyfish,
bright enough to light the dark,

and that butterfly
still alive on my arm,
eager for another day,

and I feel my troubles
unzipped just a little,

and that seed of hope
budding in my pocket.

And it's not like I get
all happy ending-ish
and ride off into the sunset
or some crap like that.

But I do feel like I have a choice.
Like a fork in the road or whatever.

I just hope 937 Things to Do Instead are enough.

Because to tell you the truth,
I could go either way.

AUTHOR'S NOTE

I knew from the very beginning that the question would come up eventually.

So where did you get the idea for your book?

And I knew when the time came, I'd have two choices. To give some vague, veiled answer. Or to tell the truth. But the truth doesn't belong to me. It belongs to my daughter. And it is only with her blessing that I share it.

Like Kenna, my daughter found herself surrounded by cutting as early as the sixth grade. She tried it, experimentally at first, but was soon drawn into the strangely addictive allure of the blade. Eventually, she was caught cutting at school and involuntarily committed under Florida's Baker Act.

I wrote this book in the year that followed.

I think it's important to note that while this story has roots in a real-life event, it is ultimately a work of fiction. But it's the kind of fiction that has a responsibility to tell the truth. So I spent hundreds of hours researching the blogs and Tumblr pages of countless teens struggling with self-harm. I sank into their stories, looked at their agonizing photos, and tried to understand. In the end, my characters and the events they experience in *Kiss of Broken Glass* are a fictionalized composite of all these brave and aching voices.

Waiting to be heard.

RESOURCES

If you or someone you care about is struggling with self-harm, you are not alone. There are resources and people who can help, and many different roads to recovery. These are just a few examples. Since I am not a clinical professional, I cannot endorse these specific resources or accept responsibility for any of the services they provide. But it is my hope that this information will help you begin exploring the power of support and treatment, and that you will find your own path to healing.

www.selfinjury.com—S.A.F.E. Alternatives is a nationally recognized treatment approach, professional network, and educational resource base that is committed to helping you and others achieve an end to self-injurious behavior.

1-800-DON'T-CUT—S.A.F.E Alternatives referral line.

www.twloha.com—To Write Love On Her Arms is a nonprofit movement dedicated to presenting hope and finding help for people struggling with depression, addiction, self-injury, and suicide.

www.recoveryourlife.com—Recover Your Life is one of the largest self-harm support communities on the internet, welcoming and supporting people who struggle with self-harm and other issues such as eating disorders, mental health issues, abuse, and more.

www.selfharm.net—One of the most comprehensive sources of self-injury information on the web, including definitions, explanations of why, etiology and demographics, and an in-depth self-help section.

1-800-SUICIDE—National hotline for people contemplating suicide.

ACKNOWLEDGMENTS

I am thankful to my daughter, Jacquie, for sharing her story and lending her natural editorial instincts to this project, for making sure the words rang true, and for prying my most beloved and stupid metaphors out of the manuscript before I embarrassed myself.

To my son, Ben, for inspiring my earlier work, for opening up conference doors where I learned how to bring audiences to their feet, and for never letting me off the hook about actually finishing a book one day.

To my husband, Larry, for handling countless loads of laundry and dishes and dinners while I sank into my story, and for listening to my endless manuscript rants about how *I-love-it-I-hate-it-I-love-it-I-hate-it!* Even in the middle of a Michigan game.

To my parents, Jerry and Jacquie Frissell, for raising me to listen, learn, and love. And especially to my mom, for believing in me . . . *always*.

To my sister Carolyn Schiffner, for a lifetime of closeness, for buckling up on this wild ride, and for creating my rockin' website.

To my aunt Madeleine Van Hecke, for being my sounding board even at the deep end.

To my friends Karen Hutto and Mark Snyder, for the precious gift of time.

To my mentors—

Lee Bennett Hopkins, who gave me heart.

Sonya Sones, who gave me courage.

Joyce Sweeney, who gave me brains.

To Charles Egita for his magical salad.

To my Sisters in Verse for their support at Highlights.

And to all my critique group partners who have made me a better writer, especially—

Karen Bachman, Susan Banghart, Nancy J. Cavanaugh, Michele Ivy Davis, Peggy Robbins Janousky, Sue LaNeve, Cristy Carrington Lewis, and Rob Sanders.

And finally—

To my legendary agent, George Nicholson, for his care.

To my brilliant editor Toni Markiet, for her trust.

And to the serendipity of Alex Flinn, for bringing us together.

But most of all—

To the subtle hand of God,

for touching my words.